Paws, Hoofs, and Wings

Animal Heroes of the San Diego Zoo

By Shari Lyon

Art by Christina Wald

Blue Sneaker Press

Blue Sneaker Press

Paws, Hoofs, and Wings was published by Blue Sneaker Press. Blue Sneaker works with authors, illustrators, nonprofit organizations, and corporations to publish children's books that engage, entertain, and educate children on subjects that affect our world. Blue Sneaker Press is an imprint of Southwestern Publishing Group, Inc., 2451 Atrium Way, Nashville, TN 37214. Southwestern Publishing Group is a wholly owned subsidiary of Southwestern/Great American, Inc., Nashville, TN.

Southwestern Publishing Group, Inc.
www.swpublishinggroup.com • 800-358-0560

Christopher G. Capen, President
Carrie Hasler, Development Director, Blue Sneaker Press
Kristin Connelly, Managing Editor
Vicky Shea, Senior Art Director

ISBN: 978-1-943198-02-3
Library of Congress Control Number: 2015956078
Printed in China
10 9 8 7 6 5 4 3 2

To honor all of the old storytellers and the enduring vision that created the San Diego Zoo, we dedicate this book to Speed, a Galápagos tortoise that came to the Zoo in 1933. When Speed arrived he was already an adult. No one knows his exact age, but he was thought to be older than 150 when he died in 2015. Speed weighed more than 500 pounds, loved having his neck scratched by his keepers, and was fond of treats that were red or orange, like tomatoes and melons.

—Shari and Christina

Speed, an old tortoise, munched on a melon before bedtime just like he did every night, but this night, he got a surprise. A young orangutan fell—*plop!*—at his feet.

Speed blinked his eyes. "Well, hello there, little lady. Nice of you to drop in."

"Oops," said the orangutan. "I'm on an adventure. I saw you eating that melon from up in the trees, and well, it looked so good. But then the tree branch broke, and here I am. Ta-dah!"

Speed chuckled.

The little orangutan looked around. "But now I think I am lost."

"Well, you are not *very* lost," Speed assured her. "You're still at the San Diego Zoo. I'm Speed, and if I didn't know better, I'd think you were Maggie, an old friend of mine."

"Nope, I'm Pongo. Who's Maggie? Does she live here?"

"Many years ago, she did," the old tortoise recalled. "Maggie liked to climb around in the trees too, but her favorite thing to do was ride in her keeper's car!"

Pongo's eyes sparkled. "Fun! I wish I could ride in a car back to my mother."

"Well, I don't have a car," Speed said, "but you can ride on my shell." He crouched down to make it easier for Pongo to climb up. "We can go on a new adventure."

"I love adventures!" Pongo said.

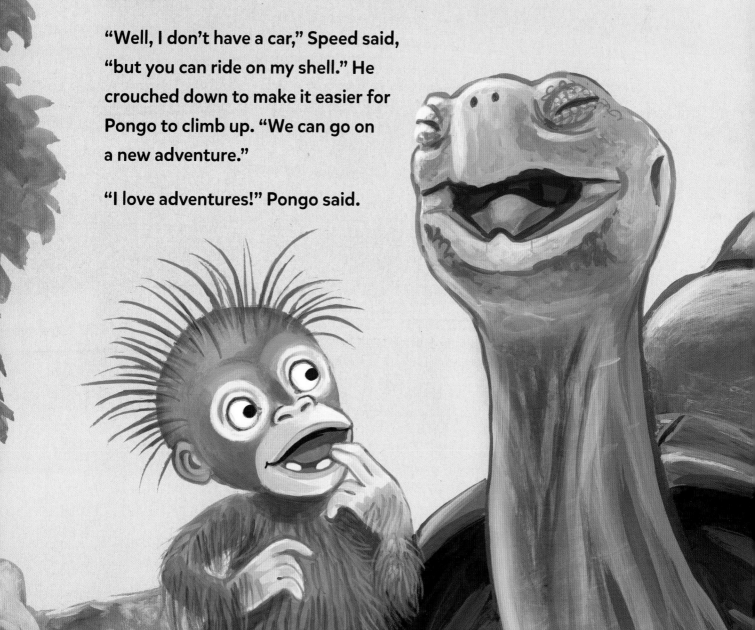

Suddenly they heard a loud roar. "Wh-what was that?" she asked with wide eyes.

"Oh, there's no need to be afraid," Speed told her gently. "That's just a lion doing what lions do. They roar. In fact, that's how this zoo got started. Hop on. I'll tell you about it while I take you home."

Pongo crawled up onto Speed's shell. As he walked, he sang to her so she wouldn't be afraid.

"Paws, hoofs, and wings,
Wings, hoofs, and paws.
Which one are you, and how did you
    come to the Zoo?
Did you walk, or did you run?
Were you looking for friends or just some fun?
Paws, hoofs, and wings,
Wings, hoofs, and paws.
We're glad that you are here at the Zoo."

"The Zoo's story started when a lonely lion roared," Speed began. "A doctor who loved animals, Dr. Harry Wegeforth, heard Rex, a lion, roaring inside a cage. That's the way zoos used to keep animals."

Speed moved on down the path. "The doctor wanted to help the lion, so he started a new kind of zoo where Rex would have a big place to live."

"With rocks to climb on?" Pongo asked.

"Yes, rocks and open space where Rex could be with other lions," Speed answered.

"Dr. Harry built habitats for other animals too, like Caesar the bear," Speed continued. "One day, Caesar used her huge paws to dig an enormous tunnel. When Dr. Harry came by, she stood up to show him her dirty paws."

Pongo rose up on her hind legs and waved her arms overhead. "Like this?" she asked.

Speed nodded. "Exactly like that."

"Next came the elephants, Queenie and Empress, who came to San Diego on a train," Speed went on. "They stepped out of the train car but would not move one more step. Then Dr. Harry got an idea. He thought Queenie and Empress might be used to having people ride on their backs. So he and one of the keepers climbed on the elephants and rode them to the Zoo." Speed turned to look at Pongo on his back. "Just like you are riding on me!"

Pongo giggled, "You mean, they rode Queenie and Empress all the way through the city and into the Zoo?"

Speed grinned. "They did indeed."

"It was quite a sight, but the elephants weren't the only animals to come two at a time," Speed said. "Our first giraffes, Lofty and Patches, arrived together too."

"Did someone ride them to the Zoo?" asked Pongo.

"The giraffes actually got to ride in a truck," Speed chuckled. "The Zoo built tall crates and loaded them onto a special truck. The crates had windows at the top so the giraffes could poke their heads out."

Pongo hopped off Speed's back and climbed up a tree next to the Reptile House so she could be as tall as the giraffes. She peeked down at Speed through the branches.

Speed laughed. "You are a funny little orangutan. I think you would have liked our first koalas, Snugglepot and Cuddlepie. Children from Sydney, Australia, sent them to us on a ship."

"I bet the koalas missed being outside in the trees while they were on the ship," Pongo said.

"They did, so their keeper took them for long walks on the ship's deck. They put their paws around their keeper's arms and hung on to him just like he was a eucalyptus tree."

Pongo jumped back onto Speed's shell. She looked up at the stars and listened to him hum his song. Before long, she heard a splash. "Oops! Did you step in a puddle?" Pongo asked.

"Maybe I did!" Speed answered. "That splash reminds me of our first hippopotamus, Puddles, who loved to splash around in his habitat. He would do somersaults in the water. Visitors watched him lie on his back and kick his hoofs in the air like a puppy. He was fun to have around, just like you, Pongo," Speed told her with a wink.

"Another animal that visitors loved to watch was Bum, the Andean condor," Speed continued. "Bum and his keeper, Karl, did a trick together. When Karl lay down in the condor's habitat, Bum stood on Karl's tummy. Then Bum stretched out his giant wings until they looked like a huge black umbrella."

"How fun!" said Pongo.

"Yes, Bum taught the Zoo things, too. No Andean condor had ever hatched in a zoo in the United States until Bum and his mate raised their very first chick. The Zoo learned a lot from watching this condor family."

Pongo sat up. She could see something ahead that looked like a sleeping bird. "Is that Bum?" she asked.

Speed squinted his old eyes until he saw the bird too. "Oh, that's my pal King Tut."

Pongo ran ahead, climbed up the tall perch, and put her nose close to the cockatoo. "Hi, your majesty," she said. But King Tut didn't even tweet.

"That's just a statue of him," Speed said. "King Tut used to greet visitors who came by his perch at Flamingo Lagoon. When they said *hello*, he'd fluff up his salmon-colored crest and answer with a whistle or a wing-flapping dance."

Speed laughed as the little orangutan stood next to the statue and flapped her arms like they were wings.

Pongo slid down King Tut's perch and climbed back onto Speed. She leaned her sleepy head against Speed's smooth shell as they moved on into the last quiet of the night.

While Speed hummed his song, Pongo pictured her new animal friends with their paws, hoofs, and wings playing in her mind. She was sound asleep when Speed said, "You know, it's been a great 100 years." Then they turned onto Orangutan Trail.

By the time Speed saw the morning sunbeams through the trees, Pongo was back home with her mother. "I'm home already? Is our adventure over?" Pongo asked Speed.

"Well, it is for now, but that is what's so good about adventures," Speed said. "When one ends, another one begins. Look, here come our guests!"

Sure enough, a child was looking at Pongo and her
mother. Speed winked at Pongo, and then they
sang their song for the first guest of the day.

"Paws, hoofs, and wings,

Wings, hoofs, and paws.

Which one are you, and how did you come to the Zoo?

Did you walk, or did you run?

Were you looking for friends or just some fun?

Paws, hoofs, and wings,

Wings, hoofs, and paws.

We're glad that you are here at the Zoo."

Paws, Hoofs, and Wings

Words & Music by Shari Lyon

San Diego Zoo's Animal Hero Fun Facts

PRINCE: It was Rex the lion that gave Dr. Harry Wegeforth the idea to start the Zoo in 1916. In 1923 the open-air habitat for lions opened, and the majestic Prince was the first lion to live in the new habitat.

KING TUT: King Tut came to the Zoo in 1925, and he took his spot in front of the Flamingo Lagoon. Millions of people said *hello* to King Tut during his long life at the Zoo, and he'd respond with a whistle or dance to greet them.

SNUGGLEPOT AND CUDDLEPIE: The Zoo's first koalas were named after characters in a children's story. They came to the Zoo in 1925 as a gift from the children of Sydney, Australia, to the children of San Diego.

HUA MEI: When the Zoo's first panda cub, Hua Mei, was born in 1999, people around the world cheered. The first surviving giant panda born in the United States, Hua Mei became famous at the Zoo and on Panda Cam.

MAGGIE: Maggie the orangutan came to the Zoo in 1928. Her keeper would take her on his rounds, driving Maggie in his car. Maggie would let her keeper know she was ready for a ride by sitting in the front seat and holding the steering wheel!

PUDDLES: From the day he arrived in 1936, the Zoo's first hippo loved to show off, opening wide his huge mouth or rolling on his back, his legs waving in the air.

CAESAR: Caesar was the Zoo's first bear, a Kodiak brown bear that was actually a female, despite her masculine-sounding name. She came to the Zoo in 1917.

SISQUOC: Sisquoc was the first California condor hatched at the San Diego Zoo. Hatched in 1983, he grew up at the Safari Park's "condorminium," where he fathered 17 chicks.

LOFTY AND PATCHES: Lofty and Patches were the Zoo's first giraffes. They journeyed on board a ship from Africa to New York, then on a truck from New York to San Diego, arriving in 1938. Very tall crates were built to transport them.

DIEGO: Diego, a Galápagos tortoise, arrived in 1933. In 1977, he returned to the Galápagos Islands to help save his species. In 2015, he was about 130 years old!

EMPRESS AND QUEENIE: Empress and Queenie were the Zoo's first elephants, arriving in 1923 by train. Because they refused to budge when they came out of the train car, Dr. Harry and a keeper rode the elephants through the streets of San Diego all the way to the Zoo!

ANNA AND ARUSHA: When Arusha, a cheetah, first met Anna, in 1980, the cheetah hissed and swatted at the dog. But soon the two became best friends and did everything together. Now most of our cheetah animal ambassadors have a dog companion.

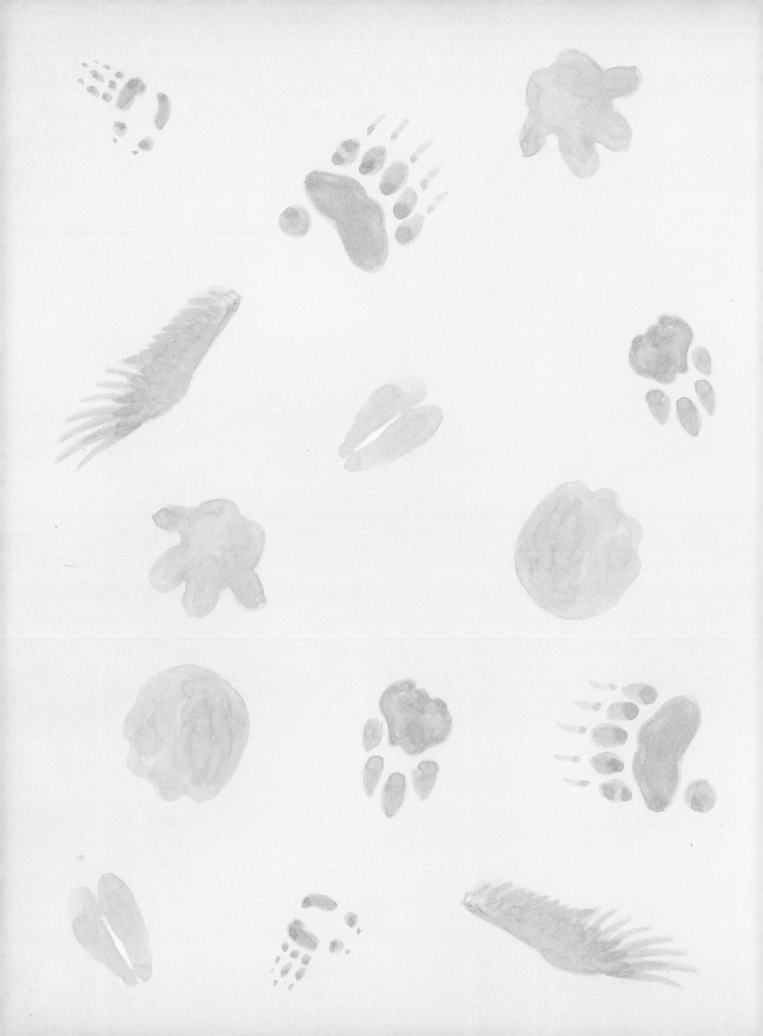